Trapped In a Pit with Generational Curses

How do we, as people, deal with generational curses in our family bloodline?

By

JANET HOWARD

Inspired By God to Write This Book

eBook ISBN: 978-1-966190-06-6
Paperback ISBN: 978-1-966190-07-3

TABLE OF CONTENTS

ACKNOWLEDGEMENTS

This book 'Trapped In A Pit With Generational Curses' is so different for me, because I lost my first book on this subject when I was almost done typing it on my computer, in my Acknowledgements I would like to say Thank you Lord for showing me that I need to just Trust you no matter what things looks like in the natural Realm, and that you are moving and working things out in the supernatural, and moving in your timing no (ours) mines. All things work together for the good of those who have Faith and trust and believe in you(God)and not doubt. We will see your Promises be fulfilled in our lives. Thank you for your many blessings and for spiritually waking me up to the things around me. No matter what's going on I must continue to move forward and Trust you. I Love you my Heavenly Father for the life that you have given me.

I would like to thank everyone who was there for me through the worst part of the Year(2022) of my life when the Storm blew in my life and kept on blowing until it was over. I knew I would've never made it through it without God and the people who God had hand-picked to be there to support me, I'm not going to name - names because you guys know who you are, and may God continue to shower down Blessings in each and every one of your lives, as I move forward through this journey called life and we reach our destiny which is the will and purpose that God has for us. We must continue to be warriors and fight the battles on this Earth, and for the battles we cannot fight or that are not ours to fight, We must give them over to God, because he said he'll fight our battles for us. If we give them over to him to fight ., let's be still and allow God to help us win the battles so we can be set free. God is protecting us.

INTRODUCTION

This Book is about Generational Curses that are in the Family's Bloodline, strongholds, and Soul Ties. How we can become set free, how we can be Delivered from the Sins of our Ancestors.

How to pray to God to break these curses off our family lives, set us free from being Trapped in A Pit. Breaking thesae curses off A Person's family bloodline, so they can be set free from the pit of Sin that we as A people have found ourselves Trapped in for Generations.

We must Identify these curses and allow God to heal us so that our children and bloodline can be set free and begin to live A life that is pleasing to God. Exodus 20;1-21.

This book will teach us, and allow God to free us from Generational Curses that have been placed over our lives because of our Ancestors being disobedient and their Sins. We must turn away from sin and turn our lives back over to God, so we can be Healed and set free. I hope that this book will give people A great understanding of who God wants us to be, and that are free to live for him and him alone. We must worship God in spirit and in Truth.

I've been through so much these past months to turn around now.

The thing that hurt me the most this year was I started A corporation from the ground up in 30 days. Well, at least the structure was done, but it was at a stand still, then I lost my complete book. I was almost done with 'Trapped In a Pit With Generational Curses" when my computer glitched and I lost my writing and could not get it back, even though I saved it on my computer. I just felt numb. I cried out to God why, Lord why? Did this happen the only thing I could hear God saying was to write it over, and once I heard that my mind went blank and I couldn't write I had writer's block. Not knowing once again God was breaking Generational Curses Off my family's Bloodline and I was feeling the pain of it all. Not knowing that I was the one God was going to use to break these Ancestral Sins and Generational Curses Off my bloodline So that my children and grandchildren could be Free from it all. Now I have begun to realize that some things are looked at in the natural when we really should be looking and dealing with things that are not natural but Spiritual.

After going through not being able to write, my sewage pipes collapsed and I have been displaced from my home, now for about 6 weeks, you can say I'm Trapped In a pit, trying to get out needing to get out, praying to get out, needing to get out. It is said God would not put any more on you than you can bear, at this point, all I could do was pray and ask God to help me through this Storm that I'm in.

Breaking Generational Curses off your family bloodline is a process. A person must begin to change their life and begin to live a life pleasing to God. A person breaking curses off your bloodline must begin to Identify the curses that are in your family bloodline.

Generational Curses in the Bible in the Book of Exodus 34;7 says God cursed the iniquity of the fathers, and their children and their children's- children to the third and fourth generation.

When I begin to write God takes me through a test and then the devil always comes and tries to kill, steal, and destroy what God is doing in people's lives(my) life it's called purpose.

Remember that Satan always tries to send his demons to stop you from following your dreams, visions, and purpose, but remember no one can stop the purpose that God has on your life but you, so only you can choose the path for your life. God gives us free will to choose the life he has planned out for us or the path to destruction, which is where Satan and his demons are waiting for a person. Watch out for the devil; he is evil he comes in so many forms, people, places, and things.

He will use people who are close to you because some people are on assignment to help you stay bound and hurting and in pain, while you are going through the worst time and test in your life, yet they laugh at all your hurt and pain. I knew what I was going through, and my life was greater than what I even knew God had his hands on me and my purpose was to be great on this earth. God is not even letting me know, but I keep praying and asking God to break all Generational Curses off my family bloodline both mother and father, those that I know of and those that I do not know or see and call them off my life and my family's lives. I will write down as many of them I know of but each family bloodline is different.

A person must Repent of all their Sins from generation to generation or sins of their bloodline,

Trapped in A pit with generational curses, it feels like I'm living out these curses as I write this book and the pain I feel for my people.' God is saying the pain is even greater because my chosen people are lost, confused, and are going astray because they took on not my ways, but the ways of the world. They still do not believe me when I send my Prophets to give a word and yet my people continue to love the lifestyle they are living hell on earth. Because they want to hear my voice I allow things to happen, so that if they pray I will answer, but they must ask me to heal them. The plans that I have for their lives my will my way God".

Thank you Heavenly Father for your word spoken to me and anyone that wants to receive it, because this is the first time God is allowing me to write what he is saying to me for the world and for his chosen People who he has chosen to give us a new life here on earth.

The things that God deals with me sometimes are mind-blowing, but it is the hands of God over my life that I cherish the most and it comes with trusting him when it seems like the storms in life are never going to end, trust me my faith has been tested just like Job who was a righteous man that had Favor with God, but he still allowed the devil to test him (Us). God gave Satan permission to test his job, but he told Satan you can do everything but take his life. The stories in the bible are for us God's chosen people to live by throughout time. The Bible is the road map for our lives and our history, So we live and listen to God's voice and live and enjoy our lives.

My Auntie Shirley taught me how to enjoy life and still live a life that is pleasing to God.

I just have to say God I love you and I cannot do anything without you in my life. I thank you Lord from the bottom of my Heart for all the love and Favor you have over my life. I thank you for what you are doing in my life, what you have done, and what you are going to do in my life. I'm so Thankful even for the storms in my life because without the storms I would not have learned the lessons in life that I had to learn and still learning. God has shown me signs and wonders and I thank you heavenly Father for your mercy and the grace that you have allowed upon my life. Sometimes I'm hard-headed and not paying attention or not listening to your voice, and I'm grateful for the Holy Spirit being in my life in Jesus's name.

God you are everything, you said you would be and need us to be, if only your people would trust and believe in your miracles working powers in our lives. We don't see the little things that you save us from that come our way.

No weapon form against us shall prosper. God never said that the weapons wouldn't form or that you wouldn't sometimes feel a little of those things that have come up against us, but that it just will not come to harm us in any way, and that the Holy Spirit would lead us and guide us. We must ask the Holy Spirit to lead us and guide us in the way God would have our Spirit to be led to him.

We are spirits and we must worship God in Spirit and in Truth, God Will for our lives that we trust God In every area of our lives. Lord God trust you, I'm trusting you to work all things out in my life in your timing, not mine.

Believe it or not, we are True Queens and Kings, We are Royalty, and the war has just begun Warriors The it that Satan has built for us no longer can hold us because God is in Control of my life(ours). God is breaking all generational curses off my bloodline, So if you choose to be set free and have your children and their children set free from all of your Ancestors and forefathers Sin off your family start now.

CHAPTER 01:
CHOSEN BY GOD TO BREAK GENERATIONAL CURSES

It's not easy when God has chosen you to break Generational Curses off your family bloodline when you have to deal with the witches and warlocks in your family bloodline. The strongholds, soul ties, and ancestral curses and sins and the Sins of your forefathers, curses from one generation to the next all sources of things that have to be broken of my family bloodline on both my mother's sides and my father's side, but it wasn't that hard to break the curses off my mother side of the family. I will write about all the curses that may be in a family bloodline later in this book.

My father's bloodline was a little bit different. This family bloodline was Royalty. My father's family should have always been wealthy, but because of the strongholds in this family bloodline, they would only obtain wealth temporally then loss it and obtain it again and again, but for some reason, they would keep losing it and starting over, because of the curses on their lives. They had problems with letting go and trusting God to lead them to the purpose that God had for them. This family was very Talented, but wouldn't really tap into their talent and use it to glorify God. God wants us to give him our time in prayer and worship. We must try and work on a prayer life, he wants us to know who we are and why he has chosen us for his glory and his purpose. We are here to touch and change people's lives, and their ways of thinking, because of what we've been taught over the years these fabricated lies were taught by a group of people to control us because we are not being ourselves if we are being lead around by people that are teaching against God's will for our lives. We must pay attention to the energy that people bring into our lives. Our Spirit is so important because it's how God communicates with us, but our spirits are not lining up with God's Spirit. Then we become unbalanced. I wrote about being unbalanced in my book 'Windows of Deliverance on Spiritual Abuse'. Being balanced and unbalanced Behavior, and unbalanced behavior will cause a person to feel trapped in a pit, a hole that a person keeps trying to get out of but can't.

This book I'm writing is because God has chosen me for a purpose greater than myself, and it's not about me, but it's about others so they can be healed and set free from Generational Curses in family bloodlines. If a person is not set free they will stay trapped in a pit and may never be able to come out unless they change their ways. I want to talk about curses throughout the bible.

 We do not know who we really are as a people, but we are all God's children. The bible speaks about curses throughout the bible and speaks of God's chosen people, the Israelites cursed by the prophet Noah, of slavery in the book of Genesis Curses of Ham Noah's son. Ham was cursed because of Noah's sons and his descendants. God also warns us in Leviticus 18;1-30 read. They God spoke to Moses telling him to speak to the Israelites,' saying I am the Lord your God you must not do as the Egyptians, where you use to live and you must not do as they do in the land of Canaan, where I'm bringing you do not follow their practices. You must obey my Laws and be careful to follow my decrees. I the Lord your God, who obey them will live by them. I am the Lord. you can finish reading the book of Leviticus 18;1-30.

Exodus 20;5 Is where God Curses the Israelites, cursing generations the third and fourth generations. I wanted to focus on the book of Exodus because God speaks about his chosen people The Hebrews Israelites. The Love God has for his People is also found in the book of Deuteronomy. I will write about this also, but I must stay focused on the book of Exodus. Where God's commandments that he told us to keep before he cursed his Chosen People who he Loved. Some people say the Ten Commandments, but these were God's Laws and Covenants for his people. Exodus 20;3-17 the Ten Commandments and Laws. The first commandment is where God told you to have no other gods before him, second, you must not make for yourself any images in the form of anything in Heaven above or the Earth beneath or the waters below. You shall not bow down to them or worship them, for the Lord our God is a jealous God punishing the children for the sins of the parents(Ancestors)to the third and fourth generation of those who hate me, this is the verse I wanted to focus on when God curse his chosen people, because he had given them Instructions on how they (we) were supposed to live a life that is pleasing unto him (God). He told us that he was a jealous God who loved his people. God overshadowed the Israelites, and God gave Moses signs and wonders to follow. The only thing God wanted from us was to love him follow his Laws (Instructions) and have a Covenant with him a covenant relationship. Jealousy to God was the love he had for his chosen people. The Jealousy of God caused judgment to come upon the Hebrews Israelites because they broke their Covenant with God.

He cursed the parents and their children because they rejected his Love and it caused God to bring down judgment on them and their bloodline, (Households) to those who hated him, but God showed love to a thousand generations of those who loved him and kept his Commandments and laws. We must not take the Lord thy God's name in Vain or misuse his name in any way. We must keep the Sabbath day by keeping it Holy.

Working six days you can work but the seventh day is a Sabbath day which is Saturday- the beginning of the week starts on Sunday, Sunday is the first day of the week and Saturday is the seventh day of the week is the day God said we must Rest, but man wants to rest on Sunday and work on the Sabbath Saturday which is not taught to us. No one is supposed to work because God made Heaven and earth in 6 days and on the Seventh day God rested and made it Holy.

Then God told us to Honor our mothers and Fathers so that we may live a long life upon the Earth(Land) that God has given us. We shall not murder. We shall not commit Adultery, we shall not steal, we shall not bear false witness against your neighbor, we shall not covet your neighbor's wife or his male or female servants, or his ox or donkey or anything that belongs to his neighbor's household. God has delivered his people out of slavery in Egypt, the Sabbath, and those who keep it holy, Covenant with God, They made with him at Mount Sinai.

Adultery was considered a sin against God and against a husband or wife because the marriage bed should be kept undefiled or pure, clean for the both of them, because when they put God first and worship him together as husband and wife you would not want to defile your marriage bed. Genesis 39;9-Hebrews 13;4.

A person should not Steal, if you steal you're depriving people of what God has given them.

God entrusts us with things so we must not take what is not ours, meaning what God has for you is for you and you must not take anything that God did not entrust you with or allow you to work and afford on your own. You must not convert or desire something with evil intentions, or desire harm to someone who is evil. God said in his word that vintages are his, not ours. So let God have his vintages on people, we are to just pray for people.

CHAPTER 02:
OBEDIENT TO THE COVENANT OF GOD

The Covenant Deuteronomy 4:44

We live in a box, God tells us to come from among them, the world system was designed to keep your mind in a box and to never think outside of what you've been taught.

Once you think outside the box you will begin to know who you are by opening up your mind and understanding that by connecting your spirit with God's spirit, You begin to understand your purpose in life. Once you connect your spirit with God you will be blessed. In Order for you to walk into your God-given talents, visions, and dreams, some of us are chosen by God, for different things to help his chosen people that are lost to wake up the spirit of God that's inside of you, and your very life will change, inside in order to do that you must change your way of thinking, you must pray and ask God for instruction on how he would like you to do things.

We must begin to work on our everyday lives as we take a journey into our God-given talents, so that we may walk into the purpose, that God has for our life.

Live and transform your life by changing your mindset, but it's not easy to break habits that you have formed over the years or what you have been taught not to be true, you must learn how to deal with the dramatic life-changing events, that have happened and allow God to heal you from the hurt, pain and scars of the past. We must let go of our past in order to move forward into our future, not saying we must forget what has happened but just heal from it because as long as you hold on to all that pain, your heart can't heal and it can become a blockage which can cause sickness into your body. We must learn from life experiences and move on, by not holding on. The longer you hold on you will stay trapped in a pit of your own making, the devil wants you to stay trapped in a pit with generational curses.

This book is about becoming free of all generational curses in a family bloodline, ancestral sins, strongholds, and soul ties.

Breaking Generational Curses is not easy but it will be worth it to be free, free from being trapped in a pit or a box I talked about being in, but this is worse being trapped in a pit because you deal with a lot of different types of spirits, these spirits want you to stay trapped with them. These familiar spirits, your friends, family, and associates can become familiar spirits.

A spirit or a demon that serves as prompts, an individual can be used unaware. What are familiar spirits that God is speaking about in the bible, that the children should obey their parents in the Lord and fathers don't provoke your children to anger, but bring them up in the discipline instructions of the Lord God.

Ephesians 6;1-19

A discerning Spirit is a gift, The gift of discernment, is having the power to see things that are not average, seeing things differently. The ability to see the truth in others that God gives this gift is called wisdom, with wisdom, you can see truth in God's word. Matthews 13;1-11,16-19.

2 Corinthians 4;4 God must give you the gift of wisdom, God gives some of his wisdom to open our eyes to see the truth, so

we can understand, but you cannot attain wisdom without God.

God also can give you the gift of discernment and he can take it away if you're not living a life that is pleasing unto him.

If we do not know God and his love for us, we will continue to live a life that is not pleasing to God's will, we are too asking God for his wisdom, knowledge, and understanding of who God is in our lives, once again we must know that God gives us free will to serve him.

God will not force you to live for him, it must be a personal choice to live a sin-free life.

We must ask God to come into our lives, God wants us to trust him, and depend on him for everything in our life.

We must focus on our spirit and take on the spirit of God in order to attain God's wisdom and knowledge, but we must ask God for an understanding of self. We must love who God created us to be.

Once we take time out to get to know ourselves, then we will get an understanding of God's spirit, our spirit will begin to connect with his spirit and we will become one with God.

We must pray and seek God because God knows us, he knows the mistakes we are going to make before we make them, but we must learn from our mistakes.

This is what we call the tests and trials we go through in life. In order to move on from our past mistakes we must learn from them, but if a person does not learn, they will continue to go through things over and over again until they change their ways or pass the test and trials of life.

This is why breaking generational curses is so important because as long as we live in the sins of our forefathers and ancestors, we will continue to repeat those sins and be bound in the sins from generation to generation. We must pray and ask God to break these generational curses off our family bloodline, by changing our way of thinking, change from living a life of Sin by stopping or identifying the curses that our in our bloodline and the strongholds that have been placed in our family bloodline and letting go of the soul ties that has kept us bound to people.

Jeremiah 23;25-27, (25) I have heard these Prophets say, 'Listen to the dreams I had from God last night, and they proceed to tell lies in my name(26)How long will this go on? If they are prophets then they are prophets of deceit, inventing everything they say (27) By telling these false dreams, they are trying to get my people to forget me, just like their ancestors did by worshiping the Idols of Baal.

These days the people in Judah thought that they would escape the curses that were placed upon their lives. They listened to false teaching by the false prophets and continued to sin without knowing that by listening to their false teaching they would suffer consequences that they would face if they kept on listening to the false prophets. The prophet Jeremiah was told by God who demanded that the people stop listening to these false teachings they will have to pay a price for their sins and their ancestors' sins, until a person breaks these curses off their life they will stay bound and in a box trapped in a pit of evil spirits. psalm 22;27-31.Psalm 23;46.

God understands our pain and what we are going through so why not trust him, Jesus has experienced the same conditions, We were suffering while he was on the earth, and Jesus also had to face death, by dying on the cross for our sins. Jesus's Righteousness acts will be told to those not yet born. They will hear about everything he has done. The whole earth will acknowledge God and return to him.

The Bible says every knee is going to bow, and every tongue is going to confess and acknowledge God. All the families and nations will bow down before God.

God is lord over our lives, he knows what we need even before we ask, for God knows what's best for us. God will lead us, so when we fall, he can deliver us from our pain, when we fall into a pit that the devil has set for us.

God can heal us if we just trust and allow him to take total control over our lives, so when we are tempted and stumble and fall he'll pick us back up.

We must trust God who has enough power to control the entire Universe.

God is more than able to help us overcome our sins and lead us to be free from our ancestors' sins and generational curses that have been placed over our lives.

We must trust God to break these things off our lives, so we can no longer live the way our generation has lived.

We must pray and change our mindset, and what we've been taught, stop all these traditions seek God for our healing, and move out of the box. We've been put in. We must come out of being trapped in a pit to be healed and set free from all generational curses, so our children can also be free from these curses.

We must be freed from bloodline curses, strongholds, soul ties, and ancestors' sins. We can be free, but we must want to be free from all the things that keep us bound.

CHAPTER 03:
ANCESTRAL CURSES AND SINS

Generational Curses and Ancestral Sins,- generational curses- the effect on a person or a thing that their ancestors did, believed, or practiced in the past.

The consequence of an ancestor's actions, beliefs, and sins being passed down the bloodline, what the bible says about generational curses, and what God showed the children of Israel before he cursed them.

Exodus 34;1-35. The story of God cursing the Israelites. Please read the whole chapter. In the bible where God curses the children of Israel for not following and obeying his Laws and for not wanting to live a sinless life Exodus 34;5-7- (5) then the Lord came down in a cloud and stood there with him and he called out his own name "Yahweh' (6) the Lord passed in front of Moses calling out 'Yahweh' The Lord, The God of compassion and mercy! I am slow to anger and filled with unfailing love and faithfulness. (7) I Lavish unfailing love to a thousand generations, I forgive Iniquity, Rebellion, and Sin, but I do not excuse the guilty. I Lay the sins of the parents upon their children and grandchildren. The entire family is affected- even the children in the third and fourth generations.

Numbers 14;18.- (18) The Lord is slow to anger and filled with unfailing Love, forgiving every kind of sin and Rebellion, but he does not excuse the guilty, He lays the sins of the parents upon their children the entire family is affected-even children in the third and fourth generations.

Ancestral Sins

Ancestral Sins and Generational Sins or Ancestral Faults is a doctrine that an Individuals in Inherited. The judgment for the sins of their ancestors exists primarily as a concept of the Mediterranean Religions, generational Sins that are referenced in the bible in Exodus 20;5.

Some examples of generational curses and additions = Drugs, Alcohol, Sex, and Mental Illness, such as Depression, Schizophrenia, and Bipolar Depression. Physical Illness, Hypertension, Heart disease, Cancer, and even Poverty.

Trapped In A Pit With Generational Curses from Ancestral Curses and Sins, Bloodline Curses and Soul Ties.

The Bloodline Curses Started in the Garden with Adam and Eve, because of their disobedience to God, God forbade Adam to not eat from the tree of knowledge of Good and Evil, So the blood of Adam and Eve became Corrupt. Leviticus 17;11.

The Flesh is the blood, the life of Adam and Eve which caused the curse by disobeying God's Laws, which was passed down to his offspring. Romans 5;1-5 says 'wherefore by one man Adam sin entered into the world and death by sin and so death passed upon all mankind, for that all have sinned.

Romans 5;19 In Order to get out of this Curse. Read Galatians 3;13, 2 Corinthians 5;21, Luke 1; 32-35.

Jeremiah 22;28-30, other Curses throughout the Bible 2 Kings 2; 32,33. John 3.

The Pharisees of this world have us Trapped In A Pit, Controlling what we do, and say and controlling our minds with things that are not of God.

Our Ancestors did not want to live how God wanted them to live and that's a life pleasing unto him.

They rebelled against God, So he cursed them, but he cursed not only them but their children, and grandchildren from the 2nd,3rd, and 4th generation. Now it's time to break these generational curses and our Ancestral sins, off our bloodline. Trapped in a pit with generational curses from our Ancestral curses and sins.

God put us on hold during Covid-19 was nothing but a pit. The pit is God's Will for our life, God puts us in a pit sometimes to preserve us from the danger that is coming one can rush God, and we have to wait on his timing. God is saying trust him; I will trust you, Lord. Trapped in a pinot knowing that God was in the pit with us.

Joshua 1;9. 'This is my command- Be strong and courageous! Do not be afraid or discouraged for the Lord your God is with you, Wherever we go. It's time for us to move forward in this generation, letting go of things that no longer serve a purpose in our lives. Trust the most High in this season, Kingdom Building is what we do.

CHAPTER 04:
OVERCOMING SPIRITUAL WARFARE

The Sins of the Parents and our Ancestors Sometimes you might feel your energy being drained, it might be caused by spells being placed on you by someone, but my destiny is non-negotiable, my blessing is non-negotiable because what is meant for me I will have. My memory is non-negotiable, My Journey is non-negotiable. My Business will be successful, My Business is successful. Leave me alone, I'm not going back to living a low vibrational life. I rebuke all evil forces in my life in the name of Jesus. Rebuking all spells of witches, warlocks, and evildoers that are trying to go against the plan God has for my life.

God is protecting me because I cannot do this alone, Lord please protect me (Us) from Satan and his demons that are attacking and coming up against me (us). Protect and keep us God from all hurt, harm, and danger so we can keep moving forward in the purpose you have for our lives. We can no ever give up, I feel the attacks on my life, I have to keep moving, No Weapon formed against me (us) shall prosper it will not work. We must keep moving and not give up. Generational Curses End with me. I was Chosen to be a Generational Curses Breaker for my Family Bloodline. God has chosen me for this purpose, Thank You God for choosing me and protecting me, Lord I trust you, I'm fighting for my Family Bloodline.

God has kept me alive through all the attacks and Spells that were placed upon my life since I was a child. God has also protected me from all the black magic, witchcraft, word curses, moon spells, and death spells that have been coming toward me on a daily basis. These people will not stop even when God warns them to stop trying to place spells on me but they will not, they do not know that I'm protected by God, I will not be defeated, I will not give up, I am fighting for my life and the life of my family, our family bloodline.

I will not give up or be defeated, I will fulfill the purpose that I was placed on this Earth to do, I will break these curses off my family bloodline, and I will create Generational Wealth. My Family will no longer be bound by my Ancestors' Sins or our parent's sins.

I'm going to fight for my blessing, and fight for my family to be healed, and set free from all generational curses.

How do we overcome spiritual Attacks?

We have to continue to pray and seek God's Face, even though we are being attacked and sometimes we can feel the attacks. We must keep moving and trusting God to protect us, we will learn as we're going through the spell work and attacks as we battle spiritual warfare when we are in Spiritual Warfare.

We must keep praying and trusting God, and keep believing at all times, But sometimes our faith will waiver, but we still must believe and trust that God will always be there, and God is always there. Even when we do not hear God's voice when we are praying or do not get and answer that means God is working on our behalf behind the scenes, or going before us to make the storms in our lives easier.

God allows us to go through storms to help us grow, we must learn from our mistakes and the things we go through in order to grow, and get to the next level in our Journey.

God allows us to go through this, He lets things happen, and God allows Job to suffer. Job 1;6-12-2;1-7, and be tested by Satan, we never know what is happening in the unseen spiritual realm. Job like any other person who has suffered will never ever fully understand why we go through(warfare), and a lot of loss, but we must be willing to trust God, allow him to lead us put our lives and trust in his hands, and leave them there.

We must be willing to give up everything in order for God to use us for his purpose(will).

We must understand we do have free will to do what we choose, but choosing God to lead us and use me was the best choice I could've made in my life because I no longer live in a pit. I am no longer Trapped in a pit with evildoers, witches, warlocks, demons, and evil spirits, Now that I have chosen God's will for my life, I've become free no longer Trapped in a dark hole A pit that I thought I would never be free from, but I'm free because God delivered me from the sins of my parents my ancestors, and family bloodline.

We are free my children, my grandchildren, we are free from all the Curses that were placed on our bloodline. I went through a lot trying to break these Generational Cursesoff my Family bloodline, when I was going through the storms as I was writing this book, I lost myself for just a second, but I had to learn my worth, and who I really was in god, and what my purpose(destiny) was for my life.

God Removed so many people from my life because they couldn't go with me to my Next Level. When God woke me up, I started looking around me. I started seeing what was going on around me.

God started showing me who people really were and what part they played in my life. I saw a lot of snakes around me and soulless people. I realized I was trapped in a pit and at this time and moment, I realized I had fallen back into a pit, but I knew I had to fight my way back out of this pit, a den with Soulless people and snakes. I was trapped in the devil's den. I know I cannot stay trapped in this hole because I know I didn'

belong in this pit. I began to realize I was in spiritual warfare, and as a warrior, I had to fight my way out of this hole to my new beginning. I knew that I couldn't care about people who didn't care about themselves, I had to let go of people because people began to drain me of my Energy. I learned that I had to protect my energy at all costs. For months God was showing me things that people were doing to me, to hold me back from my purpose. I cried out to the Lord, I trust you, I trust you, and I surrendered my life to God, I gave up everything to walk into my purpose.

CHAPTER 05:
GOING TO THE GRAVE WITH SECRETS

Our Ancestors went to their graves with stories we may never know what our family secrets and lies, dying with all the things that have happened in our family bloodline, and now we must focus on what generational curses, bloodline curses and our ancestral sins, generational sins that have been affecting our lives down from one generation to the next generation (Exodus 20:1-6).

I started working on one of my books, and God spoke to me saying stop what you are working on that was kind of funny being that I was stuck, I had writer's block at this time so I asked God what he wanted me to write about generational curses, as God began to speak to me saying write and make my people understand why a lot of things that are happening in their lives are because of the curses of their ancestors who did not obey me and my Laws. when I began to think about the things God was showing me about my family bloodline throughout the years.

I remember as a young child, I could see things before they happened. At that time I didn't understand why I saw things before they happened, and it happened so much that a lot of things I saw scared me.

What I didn't know yet was that it was a gift from God, it's called the gift of sight, a seer.

I did not know what to do with this gift that was given to me as a child, I asked God to please take it away, so God didn't allow me to see things for awhile, as I got older and learned that this was a special gift and that things we go through we have no control over them, but some of the things we go through we must go through, but we must give everything over to God.

We must trust him to handle all the battles that come our way. God said in his word that he would fight our battles if we just are still, not everything we go through in our life is bad, but we must learn from our mistakes and try to change how we live and deal with things or live under a curse that our ancestors were under from not obeying God.

My family bloodline has been in need of this book. Isaiah 43;18-19. God told us he'll make a way for us. There are 4 types of generational curses we need to be aware of and how to be delivered and set free from these strongholds and curses that were passed down from the family bloodline. We Had such as physical

Inheritance From the bloodline, Wehad also had blessings and curses that come down through bloodlines from generation to generation.

4 Types of Curses

1) Physical/ mental sickness
2) Destructive mindset and behaviors are destructive and dangerous.
3) Idols.
4) Destructive behavior and patterns of sinful behavior.

The sins of Adam and Eve were passed down to their children's offspring, and our Ancestor's sinful nature was passed down from generation to generation.

The Bible speaks about the Heart and how a person can set up Idols in their Hearts. Ezekiel 14;3, Colossians 3;51. Anything you worship more than God becomes an Idol, God commanded us to have no other gods before him, because he is a jealous God.

Patterns of our Ancestor's Sins and Curses

Our Ancestors' sins and curses-these strongholds that are not broken, are passed down to the next generation such as Anger, not controlling your anger, or sexual sins that were in a family bloodline. Greed, unbelief, worrying, rage, and many more sins and deceptive behavior can also be passed down from one to another.

We must be held accountable for our own sins, we must repent and get delivered from strongholds, curses, and all evil spirits that are attached to our ancestors that were passed down. This is why we battled more with one sin than another, such as Alcohol and drugs. Sometimes our behavior can be passed down through the bloodline. Suicide, Abuse, alcohol, drugs, and divorces can also be one of Satan's ways to kill our family bloodlines. Traditions, Religion, and unbelief can be another, Judging and bad behavior, attitudes, envy, and also strongholds. Sickness and diseases are passed down the family bloodlines. Cancer, mental illness, Heart disease, depression disorders, miscarriages or not being able to have children at all.

Sickness is not of God; he wants us healthy and healed, and that no sickness be upon our bodies.

God wants us to be healed from generational curses, witchcraft, or as some may say a witchy spirit, that is controlling and manipulating spirits in our family bloodlines.

Anger and violence are also one, we must call out all curses that were passed down through the family bloodlines, that have become strongholds over time,(generations).

Bloodline curses are a curse that will destroy a whole generation of people. Through prayer and fasting, you can free your family bloodline from sin.

Hosa 4;6 The bible states that my people are destroyed from the lack of knowledge.

Most people are not aware of what sins or curses are in their family bloodline, but through prayer, a person can be free. The blood of Jesus can break those patterns of all ungodly cycles that are in a family bloodline. So let's rewrite our family stories by breaking all bloodline curses and generational curses, soul ties, ancestor's sins, and strongholds, so we can be free in the name of Jesus. We do not want our family to no longer be Trapped in a pit with generational curses.

CHAPTER 06:
GRAVE SECRETS

Incest- sexual Relations between people being too closely related to marry each other.

Insest- Insest- Inbred family on plantations generations old Incest may be looked in the New World Encyclopedia.

The crime of having sexual intercourse with a parent, child, sibling, or grandchild under a family code, section 2200. Marriage between parents and children, ancestors and descendants of every degree, brothers and sisters of that degree including sisters and uncles and aunties with nieces or nephews is illegal across the United States.

Reasons why you do not biologically marry or have children with family is because it is dangerous to inbreed, because it would cause genetic disorders it can cause pain and confusion, it also destroys the structure of a family causing unhappy relationships, some children can be also born with deformities in the body and will cause mental illness, because of the mixing of the blood in the bloodlines.

Incest was the last curse I wanted to speak on and explain, because most of the secrets that were taken to the grave with our ancestors, family members children getting raped or molested by a father, uncle, or brother, not only were they being Raped the girls but the boy's child was also being Raped and molested and told not say anything or shut up and never talk about it again. This is one of the most kept secrets that went to the Grave.

Telling the child not to go around that family member so allowed them to get away with molesting a child leaving a child scared for life or until they get help to deal with their pain and allowing that family member to get away with it, To be able to do it to another child and that the grave secrets that should've never went to the grave. This child that has been Raped or molested will continue to relive this trauma over and over again, just like these generational curses.

Trapped in a pit with my Soul broken and rejected. Breaking generational curses off family bloodline. The actions of our ancestor's beliefs and sins pass down into the bloodline. Breaking both sides of your family bloodline curses, God wants us to be set free from all curses. Exodus 20;5, 34;7.

Breaking the Curses in Your Lineages

Drugs	Double Life	Physical Illness
Alcoholism	Double minded	Hypertension
Mental Illness	Abandonme nt	Poverty
Heart Attacks	Arthritis	Disobedient
Diabetes	Blood Disorder	Suicide
Strokes	Stomach Disorders	Bad Habits
Cancer	Unforgivene ss	Dying Young
Controlling Spirits	Chronic Disease	Prison
Depression	Anger	Santic powers
Perbic spirit-promusic	Rage	Evil Forces

Abortions	Deceitfulness	Being-In-Bandage
Murdering Spirit	Heart Disease	Relying-On-OthersTo Protect family
Homosexuality	Strongholds	Cheating
Jezebel Spirit	Soul Ties	Incest-In-Families
Womanizers	Toxic Relationship	Hindering Spirits
Abuse	Doubt-In-Mind	Mind Controlling Spirits
Rape	Evil Thoughts	Warfare
Divorces	Negative Thoughts	
Witchcraft	Malice	
Envy	Misleading	
Jealousy	Boastfulness	
Failed marriages	Secret Motives	
Bad Learned Behaviors	Lies	
Brokenness	Sexual Lust	
Bitterness	Bipolar depression	
Unstable	Schizophrenia	

CHAPTER 07:
BREAKING UNGODLY SOUL TIES

Breaking Soul Ties

I renounced and lost myself from ungodly soul ties with, the Holy Spirit revealed things in my life, that is not of God. I need to work on myself, so I can be healed, So I can get to my destiny as God Purified me. I must keep working on(myself) one-self.

Breaking these ungodly Soul Ties in Jesus's name Amen.

A Person must break these soul ties because when you sleep with a person you have slept with someone you tie your soul with that person and everyone they have had sexual intercourse with or whomever they are tied to. So when you wonder why you feel depressed or why your behavior has changed is because you took on the spirit of others. And rather their spirit in them, is now in you.

Let's change a Nation by laying on our faces praying and breaking generational curses, strongholds, and Soul Ties off our lives in Jesus's name Amen.

Family Bloodlines- Knowing about your family bloodline and dealing with your family's (own) darkness is the best method for dealing with the darkness of others.

Indwelling Sins-God leaves them, there sometimes Romans 6;19-23. You become a slave to sin before you get saved. We will struggle with sin on a daily basis, sometimes God will give us over to our own desires, and sometimes it can cause a person to lose their mind.

These Spirits (evil) must be broken off, Rejection, Abandonment, fear, worry, and false teaching.

The War Within Us- Sadness, depression, discouragement. We must learn to work on ourselves in order to break the curses throughout the bible from the beginning of time. We must not allow these generational Curses to hold our family back from being free from all these curses, our ancestors held onto for generations.

CHAPTER 08:
JOSHUA GENERATION

The Joshua generation is the beginning of new believers. This new generation, which the church should be teaching about, represents the Joshua generation in the new world order.

This is the new generation where believers are wavering in their faith, but do not get discouraged. We must begin to believe God the way that Moses did and the way the Israelites were supposed to before God cursed them for living the type of life that God detested (Proverbs 6:1). God wants this generation to enter into a time where we, as believers, do our purpose, and that is to take possession of the land. We will be coming out of being slaves to becoming leaders and possess the land, which God promised us, a land filled with milk and honey.

The first shall be last and the last shall be first. This is where God is now raising up a group of people for His purpose and glory. God has new things He wants done in this generation of people that is rising up in this season.

The God of this universe wants things done differently with this generation of people that God is raising up to do His will and follow their purpose in life. But we must listen and hear God's voice in this season.

God used Moses in his time back then, but now it's the Joshua generation. It's time for this generation to wake up and lead us into the new millennium.

God chose Joshua to lead the children of Israel into the promised land. We are the chosen people of God. We must starve our ego and feed our soul by breaking soul ties, strongholds, and generational curses.

The Joshua generation of this time will change the world. This is not the time for God's people to be giving up but to fight and move forward, not give up or turn around. I will not give up. We must keep telling ourselves, no matter how hard it gets, we must not give up but move forward. We must not give up and allow the devil to take over our lives. We must not give up but go after the things God has promised us, so let's obey God's will for our lives and begin to do our purpose (Romans 8:8-39, Exodus 17:1-16).

Exodus 19:4-6: God's chosen people (Israel). God is saying, "Obey me and keep my covenant. You will be my own special treasure among all the people on earth, for the earth belongs to me, and you will be my kingdom of priests, my holy nation."

The danger in the last days: in order to identify with someone's pain, you must experience it. We must also maintain our own belief, because the last days will be very hard, as people will love only themselves and their money. They will be proud, boastful, disobedient to their parents, ungrateful, unloving, unforgiving, and have no self-control. They will slander others' names, be very cruel, and hate what is good. They will betray their friends, be puffed up with pride, and love pleasure rather than God. They will act religious and reject God's love. It will be dangerous in the coming days. You must read 2 Timothy, chapter 3. We must be kind and loving to everyone, able to teach difficult people, and patient with them, showing them God's love, and perhaps God can change their hearts from being evil. So always speak and teach the truth.

We must always trust God in these difficult times and not lose faith. Trust God's plan.

Danger in the Last Days:

Read Romans 1:18-32. We must understand that when we start worshiping things and making people and material things our idols instead of worshiping and obeying God, these things will begin to happen in our lives. God will turn these people over to their own desires of the flesh. A person begins to believe the lies of this world and then rejects God's truth. Maybe if the children of Israel's hearts had been right, or if they had chosen to live right, our families would not be living under generational curses. Let's talk about how deceitful the heart is and can be.

Matters of the Heart:

What are the matters of the heart that God wants us to know that will help us heal?

The human heart is the most deceitful of all things and desperately wicked. Who really knows how bad it is? But I, the Lord, search every heart and examine the secret motives. The Lord God gives all people their due rewards according to what their actions deserve. We, as a people, have lost sight of what God has intended for us to do by the laws He gave us. The people of Judah had forsaken the Sabbath day, not realizing that it had been set aside for us by God.

God's laws were put in place not to control us but to help us be all that God intended for us to be.

God loves us, and His laws were given to us because Judah looked for Assyria to help them in their military crisis, and Assyria would later enslave them. The people had turned to addictive substances and unhealthy relationships to save them and then became victims. We must learn, just like the people of Judah, that only God is worthy of our love and trust.

Isaiah 10:24: "Oh my people of Zion, do not be afraid of the Assyrians when they oppress us with their rods and clubs as the Egyptians did long ago. In a little while, my anger against you will end, and then my anger will rise up to destroy them." Isaiah 10:12-19: God will punish evildoers.

God will hold our abusers accountable, so please do not hold hatred in your hearts. God can use their actions and turn them around for our good and for His glory.

Isaiah 10:1-8 talks about the leaders misleading the people of God. In the last days, the Lord thy God will end the bondage of His people. He will break the yoke of slavery and lift it from off our shoulders.

In our hearts, we may feel deeply hurt over the abuse, injustices, and misunderstandings we have suffered at the hands of others (evildoers). We must put all our hope and trust in God, building up His kingdom, and He will come again to rule this world in justice and truth.

God will straighten out all the things that have happened in the past. We will not have anything to fear, because if we trust God, nothing will hurt or destroy us. Trust in God.

The fear of God is the beginning of wisdom and knowledge. The purpose of the book of Proverbs is to teach us the foundational principles of wisdom and discipline in doing what is right, just, and fair.

The first thing is trusting and showing reverence (fear) for God. Then we must allow God to lead and guide us. There is no secret to obtaining wisdom; all we have to do is ask God, but we must seek God in everything we do.

God wants us to totally depend on Him, trust and obey, seek His will in all we do, and He will show us which path to take (Proverbs 3:6). Be aware when God disciplines His people; it is not because He hates us or likes to see us suffer. God corrects us because He loves us and doesn't want us to fall further into sin.

When we understand that God is the Father and Jesus is one and the same, we will begin to understand that our Heavenly Father loves us and has our best interest in mind as He disciplines us.

We must not lose sight of what God is trying to do in our lives. We can all be influenced by our environment, and we will become like our friends. That's why God keeps warning us to stay away from those who practice evil deeds. If we spend too much time with people who do wrong, we will begin to think and act as they do.

We must set boundaries with people so we can enjoy the life God intended for us to live. Romans 1:18-32: God wants us to guard our hearts, warning us not to give in to the temptation of sinful pleasures of any kind. Sin will only satisfy our desires for a little while, but sin comes with consequences. Turning to drugs and alcohol may make us feel good for a moment, but it will cause damage to our body, heart, and soul.

Sexual temptations are sometimes hard to resist. Throughout the book of Proverbs, we are warned against promiscuity and unfaithfulness, which can destroy families. We must turn away from any situation that might cause us to sin or even be tempted. We are dealing with the matters of the heart, but we must admit that we need God's wisdom and knowledge.

The Things God Hates - Proverbs 6:16-22:

(16) There are six things God hates, no, seven things He detests.

(17) Haughty eyes, a lying tongue, hands that kill the innocent.

(18) A heart that plots evil, feet that race to do wrong.

(19) A false witness who sows discord in a family.

(20) "My son, obey your father's commands, and don't neglect your mother's teaching."

(21) Keep their words always in your heart; tie them around your neck.

(22) When you walk, their counsel will lead you. When you sleep, they will protect you. When you wake up, they will advise you about the purpose God has for your life.

The Bible says, "Seek, and you will find." When God removes our sins, He removes them as far as the east is from the west, never to be remembered again. We are made right with God through our faith and obeying the laws (Romans 3:27). We must try and change our ways. The longer we stay in sin, the more pain it will cost us. Sin is costly for us and our loved ones. The more we wait, the harder it will be for us to change.

We must know it is time for us to change and turn from doing wrong, or doing things the way the world is doing things.

Guard Your Heart:

The heart can be a complex and deceptive force. The Bible warns us that the heart is "more deceitful than all else and desperately sick; who can understand it?" (Jeremiah 17:9). This highlights how easily our emotions and desires can lead us astray. But why is the heart so important to God? The heart sustains life, pumping nutrients and oxygen throughout the body, enabling us to function as God intended. In the same way, when we give our hearts to God, we are giving Him control over our lives and aligning ourselves with His purpose. Trusting in God means we don't have to carry the burden of worry—God has everything under control. Amen.

We are called to keep our hearts pure because, at any moment, emotions can be manipulated, and we can be led by evil influences. That's why it's essential to guard your heart, for everything flows from it (Proverbs 4:23). True breakthrough can only come when we learn to forgive and let go of past hurts. What others think of us is irrelevant; what truly matters is how God sees us.

Revealing too much of your heart to others can leave you vulnerable to attack. Our hearts should belong solely to God. As Jesus says in Matthew 7:6, "Do not throw your pearls before pigs, or they will trample them under their feet and turn and tear you to pieces." In other words, be discerning with your heart, sharing it only with those who value it in the way God intends.

Prayer is one of the most powerful weapons we have, equipping us for the battles that come in various forms. As Ephesians 6:10-18 teaches, we must put on the whole armor of God to stand firm in these last days. Guarding our hearts is part of that armor, allowing us to resist temptation and remain faithful to God's truth.

CHAPTER 09:
THE LAMB AND THE 144,000

144,000 The Tribes of Israel

In the book of Revelation 7:1-10, it speaks about the 144,000, which represent the 12 Tribes of Israel. These Tribes will always be protected. Growing up, I often heard pastors teach that only the 144,000 would be saved. However, while the 12 Tribes are indeed saved by God to build up His Kingdom in the last days, they will also play a crucial role in helping all humanity. The 144,000, representing the 12 Tribes, serve a higher purpose: bringing all people back to serving God. These Tribes will have the seal of God on their foreheads, as described in Revelation 14:4. God redeemed the 144,000 from the earth. They have kept themselves pure, like virgins. These were men who never defiled their bodies, never lied, and remained blameless, pure, and clean (Revelation 7:4-8).

The Tribes of Israel, 144,000:

1. Tribe of Judah – 12,000

2. Tribe of Reuben – 12,000

3. Tribe of Gad – 12,000

4. Tribe of Asher – 12,000

5. Tribe of Naphtali – 12,000

6. Tribe of Manasseh – 12,000

7. Tribe of Simeon – 12,000

8. Tribe of Levi – 12,000

9. Tribe of Issachar – 12,000

10. Tribe of Zebulun – 12,000

11. Tribe of Joseph – 12,000

12. Tribe of Benjamin – 12,000

I've gone over this many times while writing, and God finally revealed it to me this way. We are living in the last days, where men are lovers of themselves rather than lovers of God. Romans 1:18-32 discusses God's anger at the sin in this world. The Bible talks about the wickedness in people's hearts and why God is angry, abandoning them to their shameful desires (a reprobate mind), turning them over to their sins, and allowing them to live completely out of control. This is similar to how our ancestors acted when God cursed the bloodline from one generation to the third and fourth because they were wicked and refused to turn from their sins.

While writing about the 144,000 Tribes that God has called, I was reminded of the 7,000 that God did not call out—those who did not bow to Baal. These were also men, and we must remember that we were never meant to shy away from speaking about the 12 Tribes of Israel. Thankfully, we now have freedom of speech to teach and speak the Truth.

We must teach God's Truth. Romans 12 teaches us to give ourselves (our lives) over to God and not follow the behaviors or customs of this world. We are living in the last days, and the nations are falling, as described in Revelation 14:8-13. It speaks of Babylon, the great city that has fallen because it made all the nations of the world drink the wine of her passionate immorality. Anyone who worships the Beast, its statue, or accepts the mark on their forehead or hand will drink the wine of God's anger poured into His cup of wrath.

The greatest nations will fall, the strongest nations will fall, and the weak nations will rise in the end times. God is calling us to trust in Him, and He will bring an end to all the suffering in the world.

CHAPTER 10:
JEZEBEL SPIRIT

The Jezebel spirit operates through various types of spells.

A Jezebel spirit embodies witchcraft, alongside the spirits of witchcraft and warlock.

The Jezebel spirit is sociopathic; it gains power by destroying others through manipulation and control. There exists a threefold demonic cord connected to this cunning and seductive spirit within Satan's kingdom.

These spirits are notorious for taking down pastors, prophets, and ministers, as well as destroying churches, companies, relationships, and marriages. They can drive people to commit suicide and even murder.

The wickedness in Satan's kingdom is marked by various levels of evil, as noted in Matthew 12:43. These spirits operate in a predictable manner—intelligent, cunning, and seductive. They love to break up good and godly relationships. The threefold demonic cord consists of Jezebel, her daughter Athaliah, and her sister Delilah. Athaliah, also known as Alaziah in the Old Testament, is the daughter of Ahab and Jezebel and the wife of Jehoash, the King of Judah (2 Kings 11:1-3). The life of Athaliah is further detailed in 2 Kings 8:16, 11:16, and 2 Chronicles 22:10, 23:15.

These women will go after your present and your future, attempting to seize your spirit, your promises, and the calling that God has placed on your life. This brings me to the story of Samson and Delilah, where Samson's self-deceptive ways lead him into Delilah's trap.

I want to discuss self-deception, but first, let me recount the story of Samson and Delilah. Delilah was paid to deceive Samson by pretending to love him. Samson's weakness was Delilah, who was sent to discover the secret of his strength. Ultimately, he fell in love with her, and she persistently tried to coax him into revealing his secret. Samson eventually disclosed that his strength resided in his hair.

Only then was Delilah able to deceive him and turn him over to the Philistines, who sought to destroy him. Delilah loved money more than her relationship with Samson; she was the sister of Jezebel, the queen of deception. Delilah did not desire a true relationship with Samson; she merely wanted to drain him of his strength and purpose.

Self-Deception

Self-deception is the action of allowing oneself to believe that a false or unvalidated feeling, ideal, or situation is true. An example of self-deception is making excuses for others or ourselves, refusing to accept responsibility for our actions, always blaming others, avoiding reality, and sidestepping things that truly hurt us. It often manifests as defensiveness and seeing others as threats when they challenge us.

Self-deception, or self-denial, involves lying to ourselves as an act of self-defense or enhancement, allowing us to maintain false or unvalidated beliefs. Psychologically, other terms for self-deception include misconception, misbelief, fantasy, hallucination, and illusion. This form of self-deception can lead to mental illness if a person cannot face reality, potentially resulting in delusions and hallucinations.

Self-deception can also create social problems; a self-deceiving person may struggle in relationships and make poor decisions. Psychological manipulation can lead people to deceive themselves into believing things they don't want to confront. Omission, dissolution, half-truths, blatant lies, and white lies can be very misleading and deceitful. Most politicians are often viewed as deceitful individuals.

A self-deceiving person can be dangerous (Judges 16:4). We must ask God to protect us from self-destruction. Setting boundaries is essential, as having a good heart can sometimes lead to self-deception (Galatians 6:7-10).

Escaping self-deception is challenging; we cannot escape our wrongdoings because we reap what we sow, whether good or bad.

Self-deception is exemplified by Samson's experience with Delilah, Jezebel's sister. Delilah was an immoral woman who deceived Samson to get what she wanted. Jezebel and her daughter were also immoral women. The opinions of others can be one of the worst forms of witchcraft.

Mind control over people can drain your resources and time, exhausting you of your purpose. The Jezebel spirit seeks to weaken your anointing so you cannot fulfill what God has called you to do. Jezebel aims to stop or delay your purpose in life.

Jezebel will rob you of your self-esteem and confidence. Remember, the devil comes to steal, kill, and destroy, often using witchcraft and warlock spirits. Other spirits, such as those of greed, pride, lust, jealousy, envy, strife, anger, bitterness, and rebellion, also vie for dominance within us as human beings.

I hope this subject helps someone understand the types of evil spirits we deal with in life (1 Peter 5:8).

CHAPTER 11:
TRAPPED IN A WORLD-SYSTEM

Trapped in a world filled with so many pits and so full of sin, how can we escape these traps? We live in this world, but we are not of this world. God said that we must come out from among those who do not serve Him. We are not to love this world; if anyone loves this world, the love of the Father is not in them. Remember the lust of the flesh, the lust of the eyes, and the pride of life do not come from God, but from the world. These are some of the things God detests (1 John 2:15-16).

When the Bible says that God so loved the world, He is referring to His chosen people who live in this world—human beings. We live in this world; God made us for His glory. If unbelievers continue to love the things of this world, it will cripple their spiritual growth. The term "world" in the Bible refers to this evil system that Satan tries to use to lead us away from God and into sin. Satan seeks to build up his evil kingdom. The Bible says we wrestle not against flesh and blood, but against principalities, against powers, against the rulers of darkness of this world, and against spiritual wickedness in high places (Ephesians 6:12). I break down this scripture in my first book, Windows of Deliverance on Spiritual Abuse.

In the book of Ephesians, Paul reminds the church of Ephesus to be spiritually strong. He emphasizes that their offensive and defensive armor is spiritual and that their enemy is a spiritual one—evil spirits. Our struggles are not against flesh and blood, but against the powers of this world and the forces of darkness.

The real war is not against people, but against demonic forces. We must not fall into the trap of thinking that people are always our enemies. In reality, what is often called a demon is actually our flesh, our sinful nature (Romans 8:9-17).

Romans 8:12-14 states:

(12) Therefore, dear brothers and sisters, you have no obligation to do what your sinful nature urges you to do.

(13) For if you live by its dictates, you will die; but if you, through the power of the Spirit, put to death the deeds of your sinful nature, you will live.

(14) For all who are led by the Spirit of God are children of God.

Even though Satan has limited power on this earth, he lost his position when he was thrown out of heaven, and a third of the angels went with him (Revelation 12:4). Read the whole chapter to gain a better understanding.

In the final judgment, the devil and his angels, along with Satan's demons, will seek to destroy the purpose of God's chosen people. We must not give that power to the devil, as he will try to wage war on God's people. Satan will only be able to wage war for 42 months (Revelation 13:5). During this time, God's people must remain faithful to Him.

Being trapped in a world filled with sin requires us to die to our flesh and slay the dragons within us, or we will be lost. If we continue to live in sin, God will turn us over to a reprobate mind, meaning He will allow a person to follow their own desires (Romans 1:21, 24-32). This is what happened to the people in this world:

(21) Yes, they knew God, but they wouldn't worship Him as God or even give Him thanks. Instead, they began to think up foolish ideas of what God was like; as a result, their minds became dark and confused.

(24) So God abandoned them to do whatever shameful things their hearts desired. As a result, they did vile and degrading things with each other's bodies.

(25) They traded the truth about God for a lie, so they worshipped and served the things God created instead of the Creator Himself, who is worthy of eternal praise. Amen.

(26) That is why God abandoned them to their shameful desires. Even the women turned against the natural way to have sex and indulged in sex with each other.

(27) And men, instead of having normal sexual relations with women, burned with lust for each other. Men did shameful things with other men, and as a result of this sin, they suffered within themselves the penalty they deserved.

(28) Since they thought it foolish to acknowledge God, He abandoned them to their foolish thinking and left them to do things that should never have been done.

(29) Their lives became full of every kind of wickedness, greed, hate, envy, murder, quarreling, deception, malicious behavior, and gossip.

(30) They are backstabbers, haters of God, insolent, proud, and boastful. They invent new ways of sinning and disobey their parents.

(31) They refuse to understand, break their promises, and become heartless and merciless.

(32) They know God's justice requires that those who do these things deserve to die, yet they do them anyway; worse yet, they encourage others to do them too (Romans 1:21, 24-32).

I have a purpose, but I'm trapped in a pit in this world system.

Trapped in a Pit Because of Jealousy and Envy

Joseph was thrown into a pit because of the jealousy of his siblings. The devil meant it for evil, but God used it for His good (glory). They did it for evil, but God turned it around for His glory. Trapped in a pit because of your purpose, we must fight to avoid staying stuck due to someone else's selfish ways. Jealousy and envy arose because of Joseph's brothers' jealousy and selfishness.

God blessed Joseph so that he could still bless his family during a famine. We must not allow jealousy and envy to hinder us from being blessed and fulfilling the purpose God has for our lives. We are also trapped in a pit, the Hebrew Israelites, due to the curses placed upon us by God because of who we are. The Bible is our history. We must not choose religion over relationship.

Israel's Deliverance (Matthew 1:21, 12:28)

God said to the Joshua generation: I will make a new way and do a new thing for this generation, for doing My will and following the purpose I have called them to. But they must die to the flesh and die to self; nothing will be able to harm this group of people. No diseases, no viruses—nothing will harm them when they decide to pursue their purpose. They must put everything on the altar and leave it there. The Word of God is our source spiritually and relates to this world system.

Satan is on this earth trying to kill, steal, and destroy our very lives, using his demons and evil spirits to assist him. He seeks to build up his kingdom, so we must not allow the devil to use us. We need to build up God's kingdom in these last and evil days. Time is drawing near, while people are struggling with sin. However, what we often call a demon is actually our flesh—our sinful nature.

We must bring our flesh under subjection, as Satan's time and powers are limited. He seeks to destroy the purpose of God's people to gain power, but we will fight to dismantle Satan's kingdom so God can deliver us from being trapped by jealousy and envy, breaking generational curses off our family bloodline. We must continue to fight to be free from this messed-up world system we live in.

CHAPTER 12:
WARNING – WORLD SYSTEM

The things that are coming upon this Earth—7 years of famine—there will be a shortage of food, sickness, and suffering. End Time Prophecy: wars and rumors of wars, all because of disobedience in this world. The children of Israel were also disobedient (Leviticus 26:1-5).

Unbelief is what caused the world to fall, and because we refuse to obey God's laws and turn back to Him, these things are happening. The government will control the people by using spellwork, illusion, and witchcraft, but do not be afraid. If you are a believer in God, trust Him, and live for Him, you will be okay. However, if you are not living right, you will suffer in this world, for you have to believe in a world that is not of God, but of Satan. The devil wants to make sure that as many people as possible turn away from God and join his kingdom. Remember, Satan tries to do everything God does, but what Satan does is the opposite of God. The devil causes conflict, wanting you to doubt that God's word is true. God is building up His kingdom of believers. We must pray and look for signs and prophecies that are being fulfilled.

We must turn this world system back to God. We must repent, repent, repent—worship and pray daily.

We must pray until Jesus comes back. We must focus on healing our hearts and allowing God to heal us from our past hurt. We must stop believing in what this world system has taught us about how we must live. We have been taught all wrong. Please believe me, time is running out, and we must turn back to God while we have time. Just remember that some things are going to be hard to believe, but please pay attention.

God is telling us to turn back from all these evil spirits that are operating in this world. Satan, the devil, has set up traps to turn us away from God's love for us.

This world system is placing illusion, delusion, and all types of spellwork by using celebrities who have sold their souls to the devil to trick us into believing that their behavior is normal. But there is nothing normal about their lives; they are sacrificing their souls and leading their followers into believing that they can have everything if they just follow them. But it's a trick from the pit of Hell. Turn back to God because they are offering people's souls to Satan by killing them as a sacrifice or destroying people's lives. These are the warnings for a person to turn back to God. Keep praying, turn back to God by repenting, and trust and believe in God's plan for our lives, no matter how things look in the natural realm of this world.

Scriptures about what will happen in the End Times include famine and prophecies of wars and rumors of wars, the Mark of the Beast, and a chip in the hands or forehead.

Amos 8:11-14 speaks of famine from spiritual destitution, which means turning away from God and rejecting His love for us.

- Deuteronomy 8:3 says you must obey.
- Genesis 12:10-20 serves as a reference to famine in Egypt.
- 2 Kings 8:1-6 shows how God had called a famine in Israel.
- 2 Chronicles 15:1-19 teaches that if you stay with God and obey Him, He will protect His people.
- Job 5:8-26 reveals that God will save His people from death if they pray to Him.

- Matthew 24:1-29 tells of Jesus foretelling the future of nations going to war with nations and kingdoms against kingdoms.
- Revelation 6:1-17 describes the breaking of the first six seals.

Please read all the scriptures I have given as references to the warnings that famine is upon the land. TURN BACK TO GOD—WARNING MESSAGE TO THE CHURCH (Revelation 2:2).

CHAPTER 13:
THE WORDLY BATTLE

We battle with living in sin and struggle with loving the things of this world. It is when we come out of sin and the person we once were that we will begin to battle with the things that keep a person in sin. God said, "Come from among them, the world. Therefore, come out from among them and be ye separate," said the Lord, "and touch not the unclean things, and I will receive you" (2 Corinthians 6:17).

There are unseen battles going on in the spiritual realm, which we do not feel or see, but they are happening today. Warfare in the dimensions—between good and evil, between angels and demons—has us caught right in the middle of a battle. Satan wants to destroy all of God's chosen people (Ephesians 6:12). In the last days, God said that some people will turn away from the truth (faith in Him). They will follow deceptive spirits and false teachings, which will come from false prophets, pastors, Satan and his demons, and evil spirits.

A part of this worldly battle is the battle within ourselves. We deal with mind control from Satan, who plants evil thoughts in our minds. The world system uses spellwork, illusions, black magic, and witchcraft to keep us struggling—trying to find truth, or even letting go of past hurts, unforgiveness, brokenness from past relationships, rejection, and abuse. Destructive behaviors and habits need to be broken off our lives so that we can allow God to give us a second chance to obey Him and live the way He wants us to live (2 Corinthians 10:1-7).

Romans 6:1-23 talks about being set free from the power of sin and how we must not let sin continue to control and have power over our lives. 1 John 5:1-12 speaks of battling against this world and how we can please God by keeping His commandments and believing in His Son Jesus. The Hebrew spelling of Jesus's name is Yeshua, meaning "salvation." Revelation 12:7-12 reveals that Satan is thrown to the earth. Satan has come to complete his earthly mission, as he will try to destroy God's plans for us in this world. However, the devil will not be able to destroy what belongs to God.

We must trust our lives to God and obey Him so we will live. Renew my spirit and change my heart, for the spirit, soul, and body—our physical being—experience life through the soul.

CHAPTER 14:
CHURCH HURT

We allow things to happen. By staying too long in one place, we cause more hurt and wounds (scars). How do we deal with the spirit of delusion? Through the Word of God—we must read, understand, and wait on God. Do not move without praying and waiting on God's timing and season for our lives.

The people in the church are no longer concerned about a person's needs or their soul.

Church Hurt can be harder to define at first if a person has never encountered it before. In many churches, the leaders and pastors are very manipulative and controlling, wanting the people to follow them instead of following God. These leaders are operating under the spirit of control, using their position to control the people in the church. They tell them that if they leave, they will no longer be under God's protection. This kind of religious persecution is abuse—mishandling a person or a group of people based on their beliefs.

When innocent souls trust these leaders only to be used, manipulated, and betrayed, it is a form of witchcraft—a violation of the soul—leaving them with scars and wounds. These leaders are trying to control the thoughts and behaviors of others while doing it in the name of God, and it is wrong. They are spiritual abusers, mind-raping or mind-controlling, and using people for their own selfish reasons (Colossians 2:1).

People who bear the pain and hurt experience a "rape of the soul." Their wounds are so deep, and their pain is so great, that it affects the core of their being, which is made in the image of God. It is deeply wrong for a person's genuine love for God to be used to destroy their spirit, especially in the case of children whose trust is natural and pure. God wants our relationship with Him to be pure like a little child's.

These are the things that the Pharisees of today—spiritual leaders who are manipulative and controlling—do in the pulpit with their snake-like spirits. Their false teachings, illusions, allusions, and delusions have crept into the churches, using seducing spirits from the pulpit to violate the souls of the people. God is going to deal with these leaders (pastors).

Church hurt is often overlooked in churches where the leaders are "raping" the people from the pulpit, taking their money, convincing them, and controlling their thoughts and emotions. Meanwhile, the people are not getting healed.

How does a person walk into a church and walk back out still sick, hurt, and abused?

I wrote a chapter in my first book called Windows of Deliverance on Spiritual Abuse about pulpit rape and church hurt. I decided to write more on church hurt because it's happening a lot more, and people need to know how to deal with being hurt in the church. They must not allow it to affect their relationship with God due to leaders taking advantage of them.

Here are some scriptures to read:

- God shares in our emotions (Psalm 33:1-5).

- God knows our weakness (Hebrews 4:15).

- God feels our pain (Romans 8:26).

- The Holy Spirit—the Spirit of Truth—intercedes on our behalf (John 14:7).

Forgiveness From Church Hurt

The danger of false teaching is that hurt people hurt others. When they bleed, they bleed all over another person with their hurt and pain, causing more pain, and no one is healing. We must not follow the scoffers who follow their own instincts and try to satisfy their ungodly desires. They do not have God's spirit in them. Adam prophesied about these people (scoffers) who live ungodly lives.

God will convict and bring judgment on all the people who have spoken against Him.

- 2 Peter 3:1-13 warns of the flood and scoffers.
- Proverbs 21:24 says that scoffers are an abomination to mankind.
- Proverbs 24:9 reminds us that, to be healed from church hurt, we must humble ourselves, fall on our knees, and call upon God for His mercy and grace. We must ask God to heal us from the hurt of others and to forgive these people so that we may be healed.

We must forgive them so that we can be healed and free from pulpit rape and church hurt. This will allow our souls to be healed in Jesus' name, Amen.

Proverbs 22:10: "Where quarreling and abuse cease."

God will never leave us alone to deal with our pain. We must give everything over to God and allow Him to meet all our spiritual needs. God's desire for us is to seek Him, not man.

We live in a world with conflicting and confusing beliefs and people with religious spirits. We live in a world full of problems, but we must trust God. The gift of God will lead us into repentance and healing.

CHAPTER 15:
THE SPIRIT OF DELUSION
IS UPON THE CHURCH

The spirit of delusion is upon the churches. Delusion is something that is falsely or delusively believed or the act of tricking or deceiving someone—the state of being deluded. These three words—Delusion, Allusion, and Illusion—are closely related. Each refers to something that is not as it seems, but delusion is specifically something that is falsely believed.

Allusion refers to the act of making an implied or mistaken indirect reference to something. An allusion can be either a mistake, an idea, or something that is false—not real—but seems to be true or real.

Illusion has a few more meanings than allusion or delusion, and most are concerned with deception and misleading rather than indirectness. Illusion may be misleading images presented as visions or a perception of something existing in such a way that causes a misinterpretation of its actual nature. It can be deceiving or misleading, serving as an escape from reality.

- Allusion is an indirect reference.

- Illusion is something that is not as it seems.

- Delusion is something that is falsely believed.

The spirit of delusion has come into the churches, along with other spirits, like seducing spirits. Once you are delivered, demons come back to see if you are still delivered from your sins. You must stay prayed up. To remain free, a person must renew their mind. This often means giving up certain people, places, and things to break the spirits of delusion, controlled lies, and seducing spirits off one's life. A person can do this by reading their Bible and keeping God's word in their heart, but first, they must humble themselves. Always thank God for delivering you. Stand in God's truth and live a life according to His word.

Manipulation and controlling spirits can cause a person to walk in delusion. A person must renew their mind, repent, stand still, and regain balance in life. Delusion can come as a curse in a marriage or any relationship you may have. It can also come in the form of a snake-like spirit. The serpent was a symbol of evil powers and chaos from the underworld, as well as a symbol of fertility, life, healing, and rebirth.

In Hebrew, "Nahas" refers to a snake, associated with divination, including the verb form meaning "to practice divination" or "fortune-telling." Black snakes serve as a powerful symbol of sin and evil, so when you deal with delusion, you are dealing with things that are of the devil.

CHAPTER 16:
JUDGEMENT HAS COME
UPON THE CHURCH

The message to the churches is a warning to turn back to God NOW (Revelation 2:5-7).

Judgment is upon the churches. Many leaders and pastors will be judged by God, and most of these leaders will not make it—some will fall dead in the pulpit. These mega-churches will be shut down, and there will be many scandals involving government leaders, church leaders (pastors), and celebrities in Hollywood. These people will begin to be exposed, and anyone who defends their sins will also be judged.

The Bible clearly tells us that in the last days, people will turn away from the truth of God's Word, and their faith will waver. They will follow deceptive spirits and false teachings that come from demons and evil spirits. Judgment will come against false prophets. The Israelites followed false teachings from prophets who claimed they had nothing to worry about, but only God could deliver the children of Israel.

We must be careful that we, as believers, do not fall into the same trap as our ancestors, the Israelites. The children of Israel were in bondage (Ezekiel 13:1-16). The spirit of God moves upon the earth. Sometimes, God will allow evil spirits to attack us for specific reasons—so we can learn from what is happening in our lives. Sometimes, it will be more than one evil spirit, and that spirit can possess a body (1 Timothy 4:1-9).

There is a spiritual battle happening on earth. Demons and evil spirits are being released to try to destroy the people of God. In the last days, many will be deceived by false teachers who follow deceptive spirits. These teachings will come from demons, hypocrites, and liars—soulless people whose spirits are dead (1 Timothy 4:1-9). God warns us against false teaching.

1 John 4:1-6 tells us how to discern false prophets. The Bible says to try the spirit by the Spirit to see if it is of God. Judgment begins in the house of God. All believers are a part of the house of God, and believers will be judged (1 Corinthians 11:31). The prophets, pastors, and teachers will be judged differently.

God's final plan of judgment is on the churches, the wicked, and everyone who rejected Him (Psalm 82:8).

It is God who will judge outside the church. Scripture says it is our responsibility to judge the believers inside the church who are sinning. We are to remove or stay away from evil people among us. Judgment is already occurring in the churches, like in Ephesus (Acts 17).

- Self-evaluation (1 Corinthians 11:28)

- Self-judgment (Matthew 18:15-17)

- Spiritual discernment (Ephesians 4:21-23)

- Divine discipline (Hebrews 12:5-11)

Judgment during the Tribulation period: Revelation 6:16, the seven seals opened, the seven trumpets blown, and the seven bowls poured out.

God's Judgment Against the Wicked

God's wrath is against sin, bringing the nation of Israel to repentance (2 Corinthians 5:10).

The Raptured and the Judgment of Nations

Matthew 25:31-46: After the Tribulation period, judgment will come upon the Gentile nations. They will be judged for their treatment of the Israelites during the Tribulation period. The sheep will enter the millennial kingdom, but those who followed the Antichrist and persecuted the Israelites will be cast into Hell. The fallen angels will also face judgment (1 Corinthians 6:2-11).

Believers will judge the angels and demons; they will be bound to Hell and cast into the lake of fire (Jude 1:6). The final judgment will be upon unbelievers because of their sins (James 2:5-13).

The people that follow God will have joy, peace, and protection, but they must turn back to Him and follow His laws and commandments (Romans 1:18-32). God's anger is because of reckless behavior, influenced by drugs, alcohol, violence, immoral sexual behavior, witchcraft, same-sex marriages, and false teachings, just to name a few.

The end has come. The time has come where God says, "I will pour out my wrath upon America."

Romans 1:18-32 speaks about everything that the world system—the United States of America—has done to cause curses to come upon this country. God's anger and wrath will be upon the American people. Turn back to God before it's too late (Ezekiel 7:1-27).

Please read: Babylon is falling. Babylon is the United States of America.

CHAPTER 17:
WARNING TO AMERICA

This message is to the churches, and also to America, because they have brought a curse upon the United States of America.

Time is almost up. There is going to be a big war in America, and you have caused a curse upon this land by taking my people's land, mistreating them, and making laws that have oppressed my people. For years, you have robbed many nations, taking their land and resources and going against my plans—God's plans. You will be destroyed along with Satan, the devil, and all his demons. I will destroy the United States if they do not turn back to me. America has brought a curse upon its own land. (Revelation 2:5-7)

CONCLUSION OF TRAPPED IN A PIT WITH GENERATIONAL CURSES

Knowing about your family bloodline and dealing with your family's own darkness is the best method for confronting the darkness of others.

I was marked to be the first generational curse breaker in my family—the first for everything that was coming before and after—so I started changing my life. I found myself in a spiritual entanglement, in a relationship with a narcissist (witch/warlock). It was a different kind of relationship, and it wasn't easy to let go of, but I knew I had to let go before it destroyed me. I was spiritually entangled with a narcissistic witch—a soulless person—who was out to destroy my purpose and my very life. I had to be obedient to God. Sometimes, obedience is the sacrifice. Obedience is better than sacrifice.

Then I began to focus on self-care, prioritizing my own life and the purpose God had for me. I had to discover the things I needed to release from my life to protect my energy. Being able to forgive and let go of all the hurt and pain allowed me to heal. Part of what I needed to release from my life included many family members and friends. Trust me, God removed a lot of people from my life so I could focus on breaking generational curses, strongholds, and soul ties to protect my energy— especially my heart.

You must start by working on yourself, healing, and loving yourself by allowing God to heal you.

I trusted God because if you don't let go of what God did not send, you will keep delaying what God is trying to do for you or what God is trying to place in your life.

Blessings to you and your family. I hope this book helps you understand why we suffer so much and what causes so much pain in families today. I am very grateful to God for my new life. My life has changed, and now I feel like a new person. Everything that God has promised me is beginning to manifest, and I am receiving the desires of my heart.

Thank you, Heavenly Father, for your many mind-blowing blessings.

Back Cover

This book is part of a series titled *Trapped in a Pit with Generational Curses,* which also addresses generational trauma.

I, Janet K. Howard, was placed on this earth to break the generational curses and trauma that were placed on my family bloodline by my ancestors' sins. The war has just begun, warriors. The pit that Satan built for me can no longer hold me because God is in control of my life, and He is breaking all generational curses off my family bloodline.

If you choose to be set free and want your children and their descendants to be free from your ancestors' curses and sins, start now by praying and disconnecting from your generational bloodline curses. Remember, your family's future generations are in your hands, whether you believe it or not.

Repeat after me: *I am a healer of generational curses. God placed me here to break generational curses off my family bloodline, including issues like mental health struggles, anxiety, depression, strongholds, and soul ties, just to name a few. But you must look within yourself and get out of your own way.*

Start by reading:

Book One: *Windows of Deliverance on Spiritual Abuse,*

followed by:

Book Two: *My Soul Has Been Abused*

and

Book Three: *Trapped in a Pit with Generational Curses.*

And *Book Four*, coming soon, is part of this series that God has inspired me to write. I will continue to write these books as God gives them to me. My hope is that through these works, we will all be set free from the darkness that is upon the land. I pray that these books will be a blessing to all who read them, as God continues to inspire me to write.

Blessings...